D1156181

A Chameleon's World

Eric Doty

EYEDISCOVER

EYEDISCOVER

Go to **www.eyediscover.com** and enter this book's unique code.

BOOK CODE

E 5 5 7 6 4 2

EYEDISCOVER brings you media enhanced books that support active learning.

Published by AV² by Weigl
350 5ᵗʰ Avenue, 59ᵗʰ Floor   New York, NY   10118
Website: www.eyediscover.com

Library of Congress Control Number: 2016931184

ISBN 978-1-4896-5170-9 (hardcover)

Printed in the United States of America
in Brainerd, Minnesota
1 2 3 4 5 6 7 8 9 0   20 19 18 17 16

012016
011816

Editor: Katie Gillespie
Designer: Mandy Christiansen

Weigl acknowledges Corbis, Alamy, and Minden as the primary image suppliers for this title.

EYEDISCOVER provides enriched content, optimized for tablet use, that supplements and complements this book. EYEDISCOVER books strive to create inspired learning and engage young minds in a total learning experience.

I am the king of the jungle.

Watch
Video content brings each page to life.

Browse
Thumbnails make navigation simple.

Read
Follow along with text on the screen.

Listen
Hear each page read aloud.

Your EYEDISCOVER Optic Readalongs come alive with...

Audio
Listen to the entire book read aloud.

Video
High resolution videos turn each spread into an optic readalong.

OPTIMIZED FOR

☑ **TABLETS**

☑ **WHITEBOARDS**

☑ **COMPUTERS**

☑ **AND MUCH MORE!**

A Chameleon's World

In this book, you will learn about

- **how I look**
- **where I live**
- **what I eat**

and much more!

I am a chameleon.

5

I am a lizard. My body can be many different colors.

6

My skin changes color to help me hide. I also change color to show how I feel.

9

I live in a tree. I like to climb the branches.

I eat insects such as crickets and grasshoppers.

15

My sticky tongue helps me catch insects to eat.

My eyes can point any way. I can see in two different directions at the same time.

If you meet me, I may be afraid. If you see me, stay away.

21

CHAMELEONS BY THE NUMBERS

There are more than **150 different** species of chameleon.

Almost **half** of the chameleons on Earth live in **Madagascar, Africa.**

A chameleon's tongue can move **faster than a fighter jet.**

A chameleon can use its tail like a **fifth arm**.

The **largest** chameleons are more than **2 feet** long.

(60 centimeters)

Some chameleons can lay more than **100 EGGS** at a time.

KEY WORDS

Research has shown that as much as 65 percent of all written material published in English is made up of 300 words. These 300 words cannot be taught using pictures or learned by sounding them out. They must be recognized by sight. This book contains 39 common sight words to help young readers improve their reading fluency and comprehension. This book also teaches young readers several important content words, such as proper nouns. These words are paired with pictures to aid in learning and improve understanding.

Page	Sight Words First Appearance
5	a, am, I
6	be, can, different, many, my
9	also, changes, help, how, me, show, to
10	in, like, live, the, tree
13	is, than
14	and, as, eat, such
18	any, at, eyes, point, same, see, time, two, way
21	away, if, may, you

Page	Content Words First Appearance
5	chameleon
6	body, colors, lizard
9	skin
10	branches
13	tongue
14	crickets, grasshoppers, insects
18	directions

I am the king of the jungle.

Watch
Video content brings each page to life.

Browse
Thumbnails make navigation simple.

Read
Follow along with text on the screen.

Listen
Hear each page read aloud.

EYEDISCOVER

Go to **www.eyediscover.com** and enter this book's unique code.

BOOK CODE

E557642

24